ZAZA'S BIG BREAK

Emily Arnold McCully

Harper & Row, Publishers   New York

For Liz

ZAZA'S BIG BREAK
Copyright © 1989 by Emily Arnold McCully
All rights reserved. No part of this book may be
used or reproduced in any manner whatsoever without
written permission except in the case of brief quotations
embodied in critical articles and reviews. Printed in
the United States of America. For information address
Harper & Row Junior Books, 10 East 53rd Street,
New York, N.Y. 10022.
1 2 3 4 5 6 7 8 9 10
First Edition

Library of Congress Cataloging-in-Publication Data
McCully, Emily Arnold.
    Zaza's big break / by Emily Arnold McCully.
        p.   cm.
    Summary: Zaza, an acting bear, leaves the stage to audition for a
television show but discovers that performing for the small screen is not
her cup of tea.
    ISBN 0-06-024223-X : $. —ISBN 0-06-024224-8 (lib. bdg.) : $
    [1. Actors and actresses—Fiction.   2. Television—Fiction.
3. Bears—Fiction.]   I. Title.
PZ7.M478415Zaz 1989   88-36836
[E]—dc19   CIP
                                                                AC

Zaza, Edwin, and Sarah had been actors in the family theater from the time they were babies. Bruno, their father, wrote plays; Sophie, their mother, directed them; and everyone performed them. Zaza often said to herself, "I have a wonderful life!"

Zaza played princesses,

warriors,

nurses,

explorers,

and spies.

She made herself happy, gloomy, angry, frightened, or mean. If her character was especially sad, she cried.

The audiences cried, too. Afterward, they clapped and clapped
for many curtain calls.

One night, after a performance of *Bear with Me,* Bruno told Sophie, "I have momentous news. Call the children. We face a difficult family decision."

Zaza, Edwin, and Sarah were still keyed up from the performance. Bruno hushed them. "Zaza has been invited to Hollywood to try out for a role in a TV show."

Zaza gasped. *"Me?"* she cried happily. Edwin and Sarah were quiet. They wished *they* had been asked, too.

"Do you want to go?" Sophie asked Zaza.

"Oh, yes!" Zaza said.

"Then you should give it a try," Sophie decided. "But we must all go. You are still a child, and I'm not sure this is a good thing."

"Oh, Motherrrr," said Zaza.

Zaza ran to tell her friend Shirl. When Shirl heard Zaza's news, she said, "Oh, I will miss you, Zaza. When will I see you?"

"You will see me on TV," said Zaza. "And you can come to Hollywood to visit."

"Well, good luck," said Shirl. "I hope you will still be my friend after you become a TV star."

On the plane, Bruno and Sophie hoped Hollywood wouldn't make Zaza grow up too fast. Zaza imagined the life of a star.

Everyone everywhere would know her!

The TV producer whisked Zaza off as soon as they arrived. Zaza sat forever in a chair while many workers prepared her for her screen test. At the theater, she had always put on her makeup herself. She had never had to try out for a part, either. What if she failed her screen test?

The family stood around waiting, but Edwin and Sarah were soon bored. Bruno suggested they go to the beach.

Edwin and Sarah were thrilled to find that the Pacific Ocean was really blue, and the crashing waves helped take Bruno's mind off his little Zaza.

Sophie wrote postcards to friends back home. "We are hoping
they will appreciate Zaza at the TV studio," she told them.

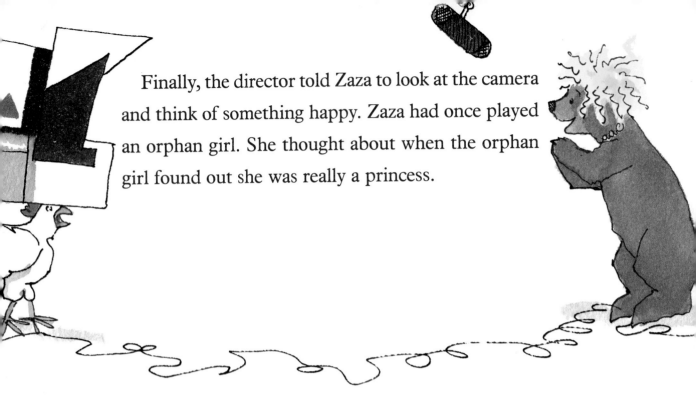

Finally, the director told Zaza to look at the camera and think of something happy. Zaza had once played an orphan girl. She thought about when the orphan girl found out she was really a princess.

Next, she told Zaza to think of something sad. Zaza remembered when the orphan was still cold and hungry and didn't know who she was. "Hey!" said the director. "Don't get carried away! This isn't the theater!"

Zaza did as she was told.

When the family returned from the beach, Zaza came out of the studio. Nobody recognized her. "Mama," she said, and Sophie screamed. Edwin and Sarah laughed until tears rolled down their cheeks. Zaza was hurt. Of course she looked different. She looked like a TV star!

They set out to find something to eat. It was a long trek before they came to a restaurant.

The food was strange, but, after a few bites, Edwin said, "This is a lot better than it looks." Zaza hardly tasted her meal. She couldn't stop wondering if she had passed her screen test.

That night, the telephone rang in their hotel room. "We want Zaza!" said the producer. "She will play the sister of Melanie Lapdog in her new show, *Melanie's Millions*."

"Only the *sister*?" cried Zaza.

"Every role is important," Sophie said sternly.

The next morning, Zaza had to be at the studio at six o'clock. She waited hours and hours but no one called her. She was used to being busy at the theater, even when she wasn't acting. She could make costumes, run lights, paint scenery. She wondered what Shirl was doing. *Did she have a new friend?* Zaza had never been homesick before. It was one more new thing about Hollywood.

That night, Sophie asked, "Are you happy, so far, working in TV?"

Zaza said, "Yes, Mama." The family had given up a lot to bring her to Hollywood. How could she let them down?

When Melanie Lapdog came to the studio the next day, Zaza rushed over to make friends. But Melanie stayed in her dressing room. Did being a star mean you had to be by yourself all the time?

At last, they were ready for her. Zaza began to speak her lines. "STOP!" cried the director. "You will be on a little screen, not a stage. Just *be yourself*."

Zaza did as she was told, but it was no fun. "I can be myself anytime," she thought. "What I love about acting is being someone else."

By the end of the day, Zaza had to admit that she didn't belong in
TV. But did she dare tell the director? She decided she must! "I
miss all the roles I played in the theater," she said. "And I miss the
audience!"

"Well, TV acting is not everyone's cup of tea," said the director.
"If the theater is in your blood, you should go back to it."

Zaza was relieved. But she still had to face her family. "TV acting is not my cup of tea," she told them. "I'm sorry if I let you down!"

"You didn't let us down!" Bruno said. "You were brave to give it a try."

"We can go home!" shouted Edwin and Sarah.

Sophie whispered to Bruno, "Zaza grew up fast, after all."

They had a celebration dinner and then took a drive to show Zaza
the sights. "Now that I can go home, I love Hollywood," she said.

When they got home, Zaza raced to Shirl's house.

"You're not a star?" Shirl asked. "You're still my best friend?"

Zaza was overjoyed to see that Shirl had not found someone new.

"You may tell everyone that I have returned to the stage," she said.

"What do you know!" Shirl cried. "You're still the same Zaza!"

But of course she wasn't.

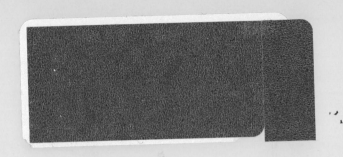

St. Louis de Montfort Catholic School
Fishers, IN